FRED
GETS
DRESSED

PETER BROWN

LITTLE, BROWN AND COMPANY

NEW YORK · BOSTON

Fred is naked.

He romps through the house

naked and wild and free.

He romps around his bedroom

and across the hall

and into Mom and Dad's bedroom.

Fred might never get dressed!

But what's this? Fred has stopped romping.

He peeks into Mom and Dad's closet.

He walks through the door.

Fred looks at Dad's side of the closet.

He thinks about the way Dad dresses.

It might be fun to dress like Dad.
So Fred carefully picks out a shirt
and a tie and a pair of shoes.

But he has trouble putting them on.

Fred looks at Mom's side of the closet.

He thinks about the way Mom dresses.

It might be fun to dress like Mom.
So Fred carefully picks out a blouse
and a scarf and a pair of shoes.

He has no trouble putting them on,
but he is not finished yet.

He walks out of the closet
and over to Mom's table.

The shoes he's wearing are big
and wobbly, so he has to go slow.

Fred picks through Mom's jewelry box and makeup drawer.

He thinks about Mom's different styles.

Fred knows what to do with jewelry.

But what are these things for?

Uh-oh!

Before Fred can clean his face,
Mom and Dad come stomping into the room.

Mom picks out
different cases and
tubes and brushes.

She begins doing her makeup and her hair.

Fred watches closely and follows along.

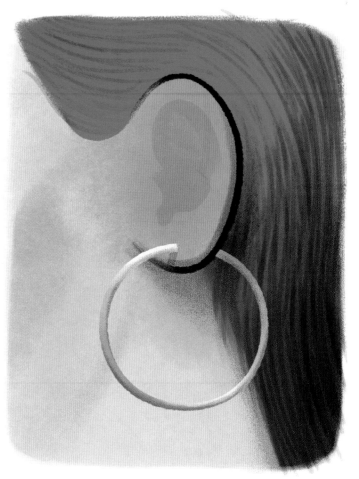

The whole family

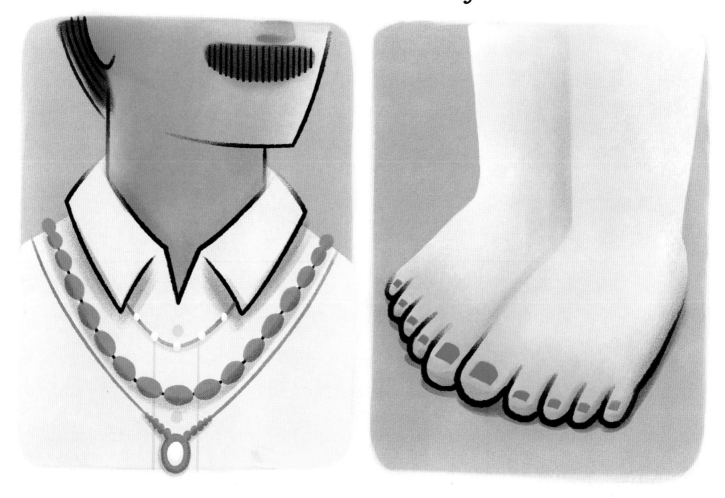

joins the fun.

Now Fred is dressed.

Well, mostly dressed.

For my mom,
who would have
loved this book

ABOUT THIS BOOK

The art for this book was created digitally. This book was edited by Alvina Ling and designed by David Caplan and Kelly Brennan. The production was supervised by Ruiko Tokunaga, and the production editor was Jen Graham. The text was set in Charcuterie Serif, and the display type is hand-lettered.

· Little, Brown and Company · Hachette Book Group · 1290 Avenue of the Americas, New York, NY 10104 · Visit us at LBYR.com · First Edition: May 2021 · Little, Brown and Company is a division of Hachette Book Group, Inc. · The Little, Brown name and logo are trademarks of Hachette Book Group, Inc. · The publisher is not responsible for websites (or their content) that are not owned by the publisher. · Library of Congress Cataloging-in-Publication Data · Names: Brown, Peter, 1979– author, illustrator. · Title: Fred gets dressed / Peter Brown. · Description: First edition. | New York : Little, Brown and Company, 2021. | Audience: Ages 3–6. | Summary: After having fun running around the house naked and wild, young Fred decides to get dressed—in his parents' closet—with surprising results. · Identifiers: LCCN 2020022461 | ISBN 9780316200646 (hardcover) | ISBN 9780316496865 (ebook) | ISBN 9780316496902 (ebook other) · Subjects: CYAC: Clothing and dress—Fiction. | Parent and child—Fiction. | Classification: LCC PZ7.B81668 Fre 2021 | DDC [E]—dc23 · LC record available at https://lccn.loc.gov/2020022461 · ISBNs: 978-0-316-20064-6 (hardcover), 978-0-316-49691-9 (ebook), 978-0-316-49686-5 (ebook), 978-0-316-49689-6 (ebook) · PRINTED IN CHINA · APS · 10 9 8 7 6 5 4 3 2 1